ALBERT HOPPER,
SCIENCE HERO

Blasting Through the Solar System!

John Himmelman

Henry Holt and Company
New York

For Phoebe,
Your mission? Explore the world and beyond!

Henry Holt and Company, *Publishers since 1866*
Henry Holt® is a registered trademark of Macmillan Publishing Group, LLC
120 Broadway, New York, NY 10271 · mackids.com

Library of Congress Cataloging-in-Publication Data
Names: Himmelman, John, author.
Title: Blasting through the solar system! / John Himmelman.
Description: First edition. | New York : Henry Holt and Company, 2021. |
Series: Albert Hopper science hero ; 2 | Audience: Ages 6-8. |
Audience: Grades K-1. | Summary: Professor Albert Hopper, frog and
Science Hero, travels with his niece Polly and nephew Tad throughout the
solar system, exploring the sun, asteroids and comets, and the planets.
Identifiers: LCCN 2020021785 | ISBN 9781250230188 (hardcover)
Subjects: CYAC: Interplanetary voyages—Fiction. | Solar system—Fiction.
Scientists—Fiction. | Adventure and adventurers—Fiction. | Frogs—Fiction.
Classification: LCC PZ7.H5686 Bl 2020 | DDC [Fic]—dc23
LC record available at https://lccn.loc.gov/2020021785

Our books may be purchased in bulk for promotional, educational, or business use.
Please contact your local bookseller or the Macmillan Corporate and Premium Sales
Department at (800) 221-7945 ext. 5442 or by email at
MacmillanSpecialMarkets@macmillan.com.

First edition, 2021 / Designed by Cindy De la Cruz
Printed in China by RR Donnelley Asia Printing Solutions Ltd.,
Dongguan City, Guangdong Province

1 3 5 7 9 10 8 6 4 2

CONTENTS

Blasting Through the Solar System!

Professor Albert Hopper
is a Science Hero.

His heroic science mission?

EXPLORE THE WORLD AND BEYOND!

He is often joined by his two Junior Science Heroes, niece Polly and nephew Tad.

Come with them on their latest adventure . . .

BLASTING THROUGH THE SOLAR SYSTEM!

Chapter 1
PIGEON

"Calling Junior Science Hero Polly. Calling Junior Science Hero Tad. Report to the laboratorium, and quickly!"

Polly and Tad raced to their uncle's lab. A huge metal bird filled the room.

"Behold! Our newest ship! I call it . . . Pigeon," said the Science Hero.

"We shall be . . . BLASTING
THROUGH THE SOLAR SYSTEM!"

"*Pigeon?*" asked Tad.

"Yes," said his uncle.

"That's the bird you chose?" asked Tad.

"THAT VERY ONE!" said his uncle. "Pigeons are the wisest and most noble of creatures in the kingdom of birds!"

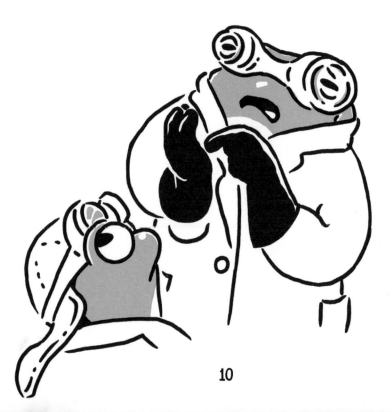

"No they're n—" began Tad.

"PIGEON, I say!" said his uncle.
"Come inside." The scientist pulled out
a chart. "There are eight planets in
the solar system."

"And Pluto," said Polly, "which is a
dwarf planet."

"Dwarf planet?" asked Tad.

"We'll get to that in Chapter 12,"
said his uncle. "They all whip around
the star we call . . . *the sun*! We will
visit that, too."

"Won't we melt?" asked Tad.

"We'll find out in two more chapters," said his uncle. "There are also asteroids and comets," he added.

"Which chapter are those?" asked Tad.

"I'll surprise you," said his uncle.

"Why aren't you answering questions?"

"Suspense, my nephew, SUSPENSE! One of my favorite things to wait in! Who is coming aboard?"

"Junior Science Hero Polly reporting for duty," said his niece.

"I have homework," said Tad.

"Do it between planets," said his uncle.

"I have to clean my room," said Tad.

"You have a robot for that," said his uncle.

"Okay, okay," said his nephew. "Junior Science Hero Tad coming, too."

"Let's go!" said Polly.

The hero of science tugged some levers. He twisted some knobs and punched some buttons. The ship lurched into the air!

"I see you added the A-C-H button," said Tad.

"Yes! The ANYTHING CAN HAPPEN button," said his uncle. "But you know NOT to press it!"

"Then why do you always put one in the ship?" asked Polly.

"You never know," said her uncle.

"You *do* know that I will press it," said Tad.

"I *do* know that you shall not!" said his uncle.

Tad's finger inched toward the button. "You *do* know I can't stop myself," he said.

"Self-control, Tad! Self-control!" shouted Polly.

Tad's finger touched the button.
"Must . . . press . . . shiny . . . button!"
grunted Tad.

"Oh, go ahead," said his uncle.

"Now I don't want to!" said his
nephew.

"Ha!" barked his uncle. "You fell for
my trick!"

"Well, don't YOU press that button,"
said Tad.

His uncle put his finger on the button. "For some strange reason, I now feel that I must," he said.

"I am telling you not to," sang Tad.

The hero of science pressed the button. "Drat, nephew Tad," he said. "You used my own trick against me!"

"Now what?" asked Polly as they rocketed into space.

The Science Hero sighed. "Good question."

Chapter 2
VENUS

Albert Hopper pulled down a chart. "The planets all travel in wide circles around the sun."

"The circles are called *orbits*," Polly said to Tad.

"I know," said Tad. "The sun holds them all in place with an invisible force."

"*Gravity*," said Polly to Tad.

"I know," said Tad.

"Gravity is like a magnet," he added.

"I know," said Polly.

"Do stop with the 'I know's,'" said their uncle. "We shall begin at Venus. Then we will stop by Mercury. From there, we blast our way to . . . the VERY SUN ITSELF!"

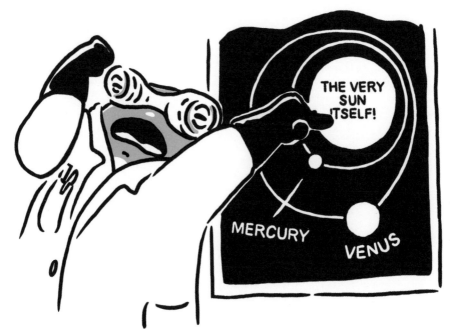

"Not a good idea," said Tad.

"No, Junior Science Hero Tad. It is a SPECTACULAR idea! We will then whip away from the sun and into the distant solar system!"

"How long will it take to get to Venus?" asked Tad.

"Not very," said his uncle. "In fact, we are here. Cram into your heat-blocking, acid-proof Venusian suits, and let's dive into those toxic yellow clouds!"

They put on their suits and floated
outside the ship. "Take great care not
to unzip your suit," warned science's
greatest hero. "It is nearly a thousand
degrees on the surface, and we are in
a cloud of . . . *SULFURIC ACID!*"

"WHY?" screamed Tad.

"LIFE!" shouted his uncle. "Tiny creatures live in sulfuric acid on Earth. If they exist on this planet, *here* is where they will be!"

"What would they look like?" asked Polly.

"Don't know," said her uncle. "But they would be very, very small. Turn up your *magnivisors*, everyone!" The Science Heroes floated in the acid clouds.

"What's that hissing sound?" asked
Tad.

"That's just the sulfuric acid trying to
burn through your suit," said his uncle.

"CAN IT?" asked Tad.

28

"Unlikely," said his uncle. The heroes of science searched and searched. Finally, the professor said, "Mission over, everyone. No life here. Back to Pigeon." They climbed into the ship.

"No, there was no life on Venus," lectured the professor. "But in science, even failure is success!"

"What does that even m—" began
Tad.

"ONWARD TO MERCURY!"
announced science's most confusing
hero.

Chapter 3

MERCURY? NOPE. YEP.

"Change in plans!" said the professor. "Turns out Mercury's orbit took it to the other side of the sun."

"So the sun is next?" asked Polly.

"Yep," said her uncle.

Pigeon approached the great ball of fire.

"Shorts and T-shirts, everyone! The upper atmosphere of the sun is nearly 20,000 DEGREES!"

"It's too bright to see anything!" said
Tad.

"Install your solar lenses," ordered
the Science Hero.

"You can't look at the sun with
sunglasses!" said Polly. "It will hurt
your eyes."

"CORRECT!" said her uncle. "But these are a THOUSAND times darker than the darkest of sunglasses."

"What about the heat?" asked Tad.

"The ship's anti-furnace will protect us," said his uncle. "It is fueled by small blocks of frozen *dihydrogen monoxide*."

"Ice cubes?" asked Tad.

"Precisely," said his uncle.

"They're melting too quickly," said Polly.

"Refill the ice trays!" ordered the Science Hero. They filled the trays with water and put them in the freezer.

"This will take too long!" said Polly. "It takes over three hours to freeze ice cubes."

"Hmm," said Albert. "And here's more bad news. Pigeon has overheated. We're just drifting."

"That is bad news," said Tad.

"Not as bad as the next bad news I'm about to share," said his uncle. "The sun's massive gravity will soon pull us into its fiery surface."

Tad looked out the window. "Is that Mercury?" he asked.

"Why yes, it is, Junior Science Hero Tad. Yes, that IS Mercury. And I have an idea."

Chapter 4

MERCURY

"There is ice on Mercury!" said Polly.

"Correct, my niece. It rests deep in the craters, beyond the reach of the sun's rays. But we need more time!"

Polly looked at the controls. "The ship's thermometer is sensing a cooler area up ahead," she said.

"Sunspot!" said her uncle.

"I see it!" said his niece. "It's that Earth-sized dark spot."

"We're floating toward it," said Tad.

"It's darker because it's 2,000 degrees cooler than the rest of the surface," said his uncle. "That will buy us some time. Polly, you steer into the sunspot and lift the anchors to wait for us. Tad, come with me to the Eggsplorer. We shall toodle over to Mercury for some ice."

They blasted away from the sun.

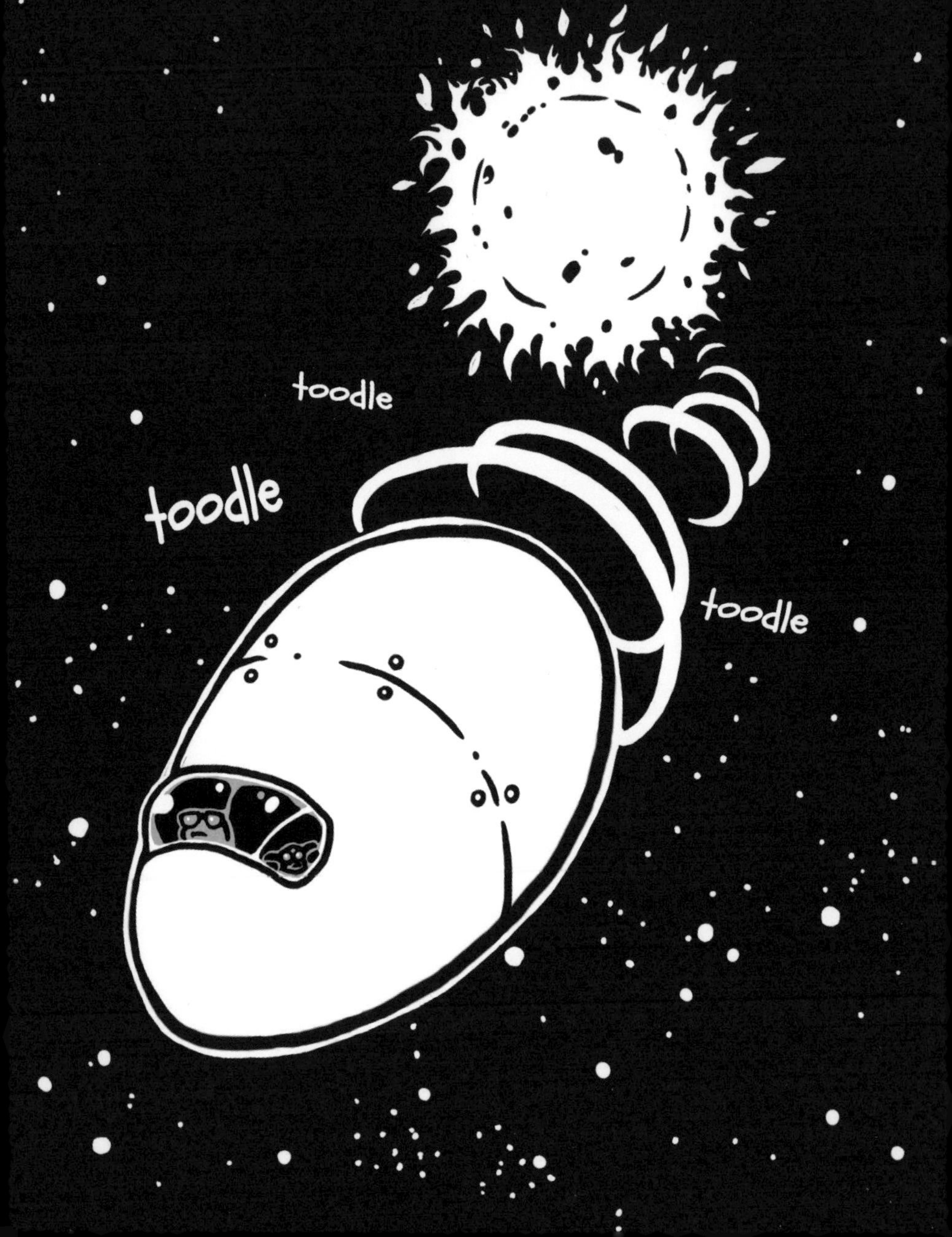

"Mercury is the smallest planet in
the solar system," said the scientist.
"During its two-month-long day, it
is 800 DEGREES! But during its two-
month-long night, it drops to . . .
MINUS 280!

"Comets SMASH into the surface
and leave behind water, deep, deep,
DEEP within the craters! *That* water
freezes into ice—"

"Who are you talking to?" asked Tad.

"Shh, I'm narrating," whispered his uncle.

Tad looked out the window. "The ground is so dark."

"It's made of graphite," said his uncle. "You could fill a TRILLION pencils with it!"

They dropped into a crater. The Eggsplorer filled itself with ice. "Back to the sun, and quickly!" said the professor. "The anti-furnace needs fuel, AND . . . I'm a wee bit chilly!"

Chapter 5

AND BACK TO
THE SUN . . .

Tad and the professor shoveled the Mercurian ice into the anti-furnace.

"The ship is running again," said Polly.

"Hurrah," said her uncle. "Now, fire up the rockets and let's build up some speed."

"We're using the sun's gravity to slingshot us to Mars?" asked Polly.

"Precisely! We shall let it fling us around until we're ready to pull away."

"How long will this take?" asked Tad.

"Well, with the sun being 432,170 miles across, and Pigeon able to reach speeds beyond what can be imagined . . ."

"Two days," said Polly.

"Yes, niece Polly, about two days. So put on your solar lenses and enjoy the view."

They whipped around the sun. Columns of fire shot up from the surface.

"Steer clear of those solar flares, Polly. The rising heat and energy of a single one could blast us into the endless universe!"

"I have an idea to save some time,"
said Polly. She searched the surface
for just the right solar flare. "That's the
one," she said. She steered the ship
into the flames.

"What are you doing?" asked Tad.

"I found one shooting in the right direction. Strap in," said his sister. She steered into the solar flare. "Tad, pull that lever!"

Her brother yanked on the lever. The ship dumped out the ice, which melted in an explosion of steam! Pigeon launched with blinding speed into space.

"Next stop, Mars," said Junior Science Hero Polly.

Chapter 6
NEXT STOP, MARS

"Wave to Earth," said Albert Hopper. "We'll be on Mars in no time."

The explorers arrived on Mars in no time.

"What is our mission here?" asked Polly.

"We are constructing new Science Hero headquarters!" said Albert Hopper.

"What about the one on Earth?" asked Tad.

"Oh, we're also keeping that one," said his uncle. "I just thought it would be good to have a clubhouse on Mars, too."

"Clubhouse?" asked Polly.

"Headquarters!" said her uncle. "Headquarters for SCIENCE!"

"And vacations?" asked Tad.

"Sure!" said his uncle. "Now, Martian suits on! We're going outside."

They climbed out of Pigeon. Tad
floated up into the air. His uncle
grabbed his foot. "You forgot to stuff
your pockets with heavy stuff," he
said. "The gravity here is very weak!"

"We should get underground," said Polly. "The atmosphere is too thin to block the sun's radiation. We will be fried."

"Yes," agreed her uncle. "Our clubhouse must be built beneath the very ground!"

"Clubhouse?" asked Tad.

"Erm . . . headquarters!" corrected the professor. "Squeeze into this crater!"

They turned on their flashlights. "It's nice down here!" said Polly.

"Do you hear that?" asked Tad.

"WATER!" shouted the Science Heroes. A stream ran through the cavern.

"I KNEW there was water inside of Mars!" said the professor. "Now, back to the ship for our clubhouse things!"

"Clubhouse?" asked Polly.

"HEADQUARTERS! HEADQUARTERS!" insisted her uncle.

Their clubhouse was finished by
evening. "*Headquarters,*" whispered
the professor. Albert Hopper dozed
in his comfy chair. Polly did some
puzzles. Tad fished in the stream.

"There are no fish on Mars," said Polly.

"You forgot we pressed the ANYTHING CAN HAPPEN button," said Tad.

"But sometimes 'anything' also means 'nothing,'" said his sister.

"Shh," said Tad. "You'll scare the fish."

Albert Hopper woke up. "Rest up, Junior Science Heroes," he said. "In the morning we leave for our largest and gassiest planet . . . JUPITER!" Then he fell back asleep.

Chapter 7

THE LARGEST AND GASSIEST PLANET!

"And there it is!" announced the hero of science. "Jupiter. It's huge. It's gassy. It's spectacular!"

The Junior Science Heroes stared in awe. "What is that red spot?" asked Tad.

"It's a storm," said Polly. "It has been blowing for over 300 years."

"A storm larger than our Earth," added their uncle. "Let's have a closer look."

"That's okay," said Tad. "We can see it very well from here."

"Down, I say! Down into the very teeth of the storm!" bellowed the professor.

Polly steered them into the red spot. The ship was tossed around like a pigeon in a hurricane.

"Pigeon is falling apart!" shouted Polly. "The winds are over 400 miles per hour!"

"Maybe we shouldn't have done this," said her uncle.

"I have an idea," said Polly. She
yanked Pigeon toward the center of
the storm. The ship stopped shaking.
"See? It is calm in the center," she
said.

"Brilliant thinking, Junior Science Hero Polly!" said her uncle.

"Nice," said Tad. "Should we be dropping, though?"

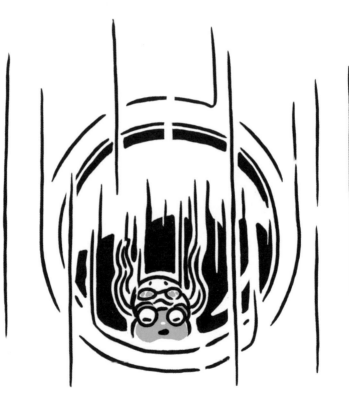

"Uh-oh," said Polly.

"Uh-oh," said Albert Hopper.

"Uh-oh," said Tad. "But I don't know why."

"Jupiter's humongous size gives it humongous gravity," said his uncle. "A gravity more than double that of Earth!"

"We should not have flown so close," said Polly.

"Agreed, Junior Science Hero Polly," said her uncle.

"So we're being sucked into the planet at rocket speed," said Tad.

"So it seems," said his uncle.

"I have an idea," said Polly. She turned Pigeon straight down and zoomed toward the planet.

"You're going right into the gravity to build up speed!" said her uncle.
"Shh," said Polly. "Concentrating!"

"And we'll blast out the other side!" said her uncle.

"Shh," said Polly.

"*Be sure to go around the rocky core*," whispered the professor.

"I've got it," said Polly. "And, SHH!"

The ship raced through the gas layer. It ripped through the liquid layer. Polly steered it around the rocky core. They shot up and away from it at the other end. Then, right through the lower liquid layer! Through the upper gas layer! And back into space, free from Jupiter's gravity.

"Junior Science Hero Polly?" said Albert Hopper.

"Yes, Uncle?"

"That was just amazing."

"Saturn?" she asked.

"Saturn," said her uncle.

Chapter 8

COMETS AND ASTEROIDS

"Pigeon is tired," said Polly.

"How can a ship get tired?" asked Tad.

"It's been through a lot," said his sister.

"I agree," said the professor. "And help is on the way." He pointed out the window. "See that comet? It is heading straight for Saturn."

"Oooh!" said Polly. "It can give
Pigeon a piggyback ride!"

They landed on the comet.

"Comet suits, everyone! We're going
outside!" said the Science Hero.

They stepped onto the comet. "Watch your step! Comets are big hunks of ice that orbit the galaxy. If you slip, you fall into space!"

"I'm going to look at the tail," said Tad.

"Be back for dinner," said his uncle. "And DO NOT slip!"

A few hours went by. Albert Hopper and Polly finished their dinners.

"Tad should have been back by now," said Polly.

"Can I eat his dinner?" asked her uncle.

"Of course not!" said his niece. "I'm worried about him."

"Oh, he's okay," said the professor.

"How do you know?"

"Because he's right over there." Her uncle pointed to a nearby asteroid. Junior Science Hero Tad stood upon it.

The professor waved to his nephew. His nephew waved back. "He must have fallen off the comet. Luckily, that asteroid was there to catch him."

"Now what?" asked Polly.

"SPACE WALK!" said her uncle. He went to the ship and returned with a long rope. "Tie this around your waist, and take off your gravity boots. I will hold on to the other end. You float out and grab him."

"Why don't *you* float out there?"

"I'm heavier," said Albert Hopper. "I will make a better anchor."

"Weight doesn't matter in space!" said Polly.

"Also, I just ate. I get spacesick," said her uncle.

"Just don't let go," said Polly.

"NEVER!" promised the professor.

Polly drifted over to her brother.

"Hi, Polly," said Tad.

"Hi, Tad," said Polly.

"I fell off the comet," said Tad.

"I know," said Polly. She grabbed her brother. Their uncle pulled them back to the comet.

"Who ate my dinner?" asked Tad.

"ONWARD TO SATURN!" bellowed his uncle.

Chapter 9

ONWARD TO SATURN!

They soon reached Saturn. Pigeon left the comet. The ship's well-rested engines cooed softly.

"Pigeon's computer says that Saturn's winds are twice as strong as Jupiter's," said Polly.

"The two planets are very similar. Both are big, windy balls of gas," said her uncle.

Tad grinned and started to say
something.

"Don't, Tad," said his sister. She
looked back at the planet. "Both have
rings of ice and rocks, too," she said.
"But Saturn's are prettier!"

"Saturn's rings are made from cleaner ice," said her uncle. "Jupiter's rings are all dusty, so they are harder to see. But we will not land on Saturn. We shall observe the planet from its LARGEST MOON!"

"Titan!" said Polly.

"Take us there, Junior Science Hero Polly!"

They landed on the hazy orange moon.

"Titanian suits, everyone," commanded the Science Hero. "The air is unbreathable nitrogen. And today it is . . . MINUS 280 DEGREES!"

They stepped onto the surface. "The gravity is weak, but the air is thick," said the professor. "We'll be a little bouncy."

"This looks like Earth," said Tad. "Except for the orange air and orange clouds."

"Those clouds will soon be raining liquid methane!" said his uncle.

"Gasoline?" asked Polly.

"Sort of. It's why we are here—to fill up Pigeon. We'll pump it from that lake."

"Our ship runs on methane gas?" asked Tad.

"That, and other things," said his uncle.

"What *other* things?" asked his niece.

"Just *other* things," said her uncle.

They filled the ship with gas from the lake. "This should get us the rest of the way," said Albert Hopper.

"Do we have to go?" asked Tad.
They watched Saturn peek from
behind the horizon.

"This is so beautiful," said Polly. They sat for a few more moments. Then their uncle shot to his feet.

"URANUS!" he said, and strode to the ship.

Tad and Polly looked at each other. "I guess we're on our way to Uranus," said Tad.

Chapter 10
URANUS!

"URANUS!" announced the hero of science as they approached the pale blue planet. "Notice anything?"

"No," said Polly and Tad.

"It is spinning from top to bottom," said their uncle. "All the other planets spin from side to side."

"Because of the ANYTHING CAN HAPPEN button?" asked Tad.

"No. And that hasn't come into play
this whole trip," said his uncle.

"That makes me nervous," said Polly.

"Me, too," said her uncle. "Notice the dark rings? They spin from top to bottom, too."

"What holds them together?" asked Tad.

"Neptune's gravity and the gravity of the little moons riding along with them."

"What's our mission?" asked Polly.

"To count the very rings of Uranus!" declared her uncle.

"1, 2, 3, 4, 5, 6, 7, 8, 9, 10, 11, 12, 13," said Tad. "There are 13 rings around the planet Uranus."

"MISSION COMPLETE!" announced his uncle. "NEPTUNE!"

"Wait, that's it?" asked Tad.

"Sometimes, my young nephew,
science is just counting things."
"For what?" asked Tad.

"Sometimes, Junior Science Hero, we don't know until we know. Now, NEPTUNE!"

Tad and Polly looked at each other. "I guess we're on our way to Neptune," said Tad.

Chapter 11
NEPTUNE!

Professor Hopper pulled down his chart of the solar system. "Neptune is the eighth planet from the sun. And it's a big one. Its core alone is the size of Earth. But, as with Uranus, wrapped around that core is a churning stew of ices and gases."

"Okay, so we'll skip this one," said Tad.

"Precisely! We shall skip this one as we plunge into that deadly soup!"

"That's not what I'd call 'skipping this one,'" said Tad.

"Junior Science Hero Polly? Take us down into the swirling oceans of Neptune. And be of great care. The winds can blow up to . . . 1,500 MILES PER HOUR!"

"Look, I can count the rings. 1, 2, 3, 4, 5," said Tad. "Five rings. Mission complete!"

"Mission INCOMPLETE! Dive, Polly, DIVE!"

"The air is getting thick and slushy," said Polly. "I can't tell if we're flying or swimming."

"It's so dark," said Tad.

"The atmosphere is too thick for the sun's rays to penetrate," said his uncle.

Kerploosh! went the ship.

"I think we're floating," said Polly.

"Neptunian suits on! We're going in!" said her uncle.

"They're glowing!" said Tad.

"Yes, so we can find one another in
the dark. Careful, now. We are in a
mix of ammonia, water, and methane
ice. The smallest of sips would be . . .
just awful!"

"Our mission?" asked Polly.

"To be the very first to do this!" said the Science Hero.

"To do what?" asked Tad.

"This!" answered his uncle as he
bobbed in the Neptunian sea.

The Science Heroes bounced in the sea for an hour or so.

"How is this science?" asked Polly finally.

"Sometimes science is doing something no one has done before," answered her uncle.

"Like floating in a chunky pitch-black ocean of ammonia?" asked Tad.

"Precisely like floating in a chunky pitch-black ocean of ammonia, my nephew." Suddenly, Albert Hopper shouted, "PLUTO!" He sloshed back to the ship.

Tad and Polly looked at each other. "I guess we're on our way to Pluto," said Tad.

Chapter 12
PLUTO!

They reached Pluto in a few days.

"It has a big white heart on it," said Tad.

"Yes, my nephew. That area is filled with methane ice, carbon dioxide ice, and nitrogen ice.

"Take us in for a closer look,
Junior Science Hero Polly."

They approached the tiny planet.
"So, you know it's not a planet
anymore," said Polly.

"Am, too," said a tiny voice.

"Who said that?" asked Tad.

"Look out your window," said the
voice.

"Pluto? That's you?"

"Yep," said the dwarf planet.

"Annnd . . . ," said Albert Hopper. "THERE! Right THERE is the ANYTHING CAN HAPPEN button doing what it does!"

"*Finally*," whispered Tad.

"You are a dwarf planet," said Polly.

"Am not!" said Pluto.

"Are, too!" said Polly.

"Am not!" said Pluto.

"Are, too!" said Polly.

"Okay, that will be enough, you two," said Albert Hopper.

"I'm on Pluto's side," said Tad.

"That's just because it's the opposite of my side," said his big sister.

"Thanks, kid," said the dwarf planet.

"To be a planet, you have to follow three rules," said Polly. "You have to orbit around the sun."

"I do!" said Pluto.

"But you go in a different direction from the other planets."

"So?" said Pluto.

"Your gravity also has to pull you into the shape of a ball," said Polly.

"It did! It is! I am!" said Pluto.

"Lastly," said Polly, "to be a planet, you have to be able to push away OR pull *in* all the big objects in your path."

"That's really, really hard!" said Pluto.

"Because you're too small," said Polly.

"YOU'RE too small!" said Pluto.

"I'm not calling myself a planet!" said Polly.

"Because you're not one!" said Pluto.

"Neither are you!" said Polly.

"This will get us nowhere," said science's most annoyed hero.

Polly ignored her uncle. "Not a planet!" she said.

"Am so," said Pluto.

"Are not!"

"Am so!"

"We're leaving," said Albert Hopper.
He took the controls and steered
away from Pluto.

"It's not a planet," mumbled Polly.

"Is, too," mumbled Tad.

"Nevertheless!" said their uncle.

Chapter 13
AUTOPILOT

"It is a long trip back to Earth," said the professor. "We shall let the autopilot take us home! It will steer the ship as we relax."

"Has the autopilot ever actually worked?" asked Tad.

"Someday!" said the hero of science.

"I don't think you answered my question," said Tad.

"No, I think he did," said Polly.

"Autopilot, wake up!" said the professor.

AWAKE, said the autopilot.

"Take us home, my good machine. We must rest our weary selves," said the professor.

I'LL GET YOU HOME, said the autopilot. The ship lurched ahead. The crew took a long nap.

Polly argued with Pluto in her sleep. "Are not . . . are not . . . ," she muttered.

Tad argued with Polly in his sleep. "Is, too . . . is, too," he muttered.

Their uncle argued with the two of them in his sleep. "Enough, enough," he muttered.

Tad woke up and looked out the window. His uncle woke up, too. "What do you see?" the professor asked.

"It's pretty dark out there," said Tad. "And there are a lot of comets. And a bunch of asteroids. And tons of meteors."

"Meteors aren't called meteors until they're in the Earth's atmosphere," said Polly. "Until then they're just parts of asteroids and comets."

"Are you correcting me in your sleep?" asked Tad.

Polly woke up. "What?"

"See any medium-sized stars we call the 'sun,' or watery blue planets we call 'Earth'?" asked their uncle.

"No," said Tad. "None of those."

Polly went to the window. "Why are we in the Kuiper Belt?" she asked.

KUIPER BELT, recited the autopilot.
*PRONOUNCED "KI-PER": A WIDE RING
OF COMETS, ASTEROIDS, ROCKS, AND
ICE BEYOND THE SOLAR SYSTEM.
YOUR "HOME." *

"No, autopilot," said Albert Hopper. "We do NOT call the Kuiper Belt *home*. Why, that wide ring of comets, asteroids, rocks, and ice is in the exact *opposite direction* of our home!"

OH, said the autopilot. *SO DO YOU WANT TO STAY HERE, OR—*

"TO THE THIRD PLANET FROM THE SUN!" commanded the professor. "TO EARTH!"

GOT IT, said the autopilot.

Chapter 14
ALMOST

The crew dozed as the autopilot made the long trip to Earth.

"PLANET!" shouted Pluto as they whizzed by. The sun still looked like a tiny star in the distance. They had a long way to go. They rocketed past Neptune, and then past its icy twin, Uranus. Pigeon zoomed by Saturn, and then past its gassy twin, Jupiter.

It flapped past Mars, home of their
new Martian clubhouse.

"Headquarters," whispered Albert
Hopper in his sleep. And then . . .
CRAAASH!

"What happened?" asked Polly.

"I think we crashed," said her uncle.

HERE WE ARE, said the autopilot.

"We're on the moon!" said Tad.

WRONG WAY AGAIN? asked the autopilot.

"No, you came close. You just didn't go far enough," said Tad.

I WOULD SAY THAT'S AN IMPROVEMENT, said the autopilot.

"A little," said the professor.

THANKS! said the autopilot. *ALL YOURS NOW. SORRY FOR BREAKING YOUR SHIP.*

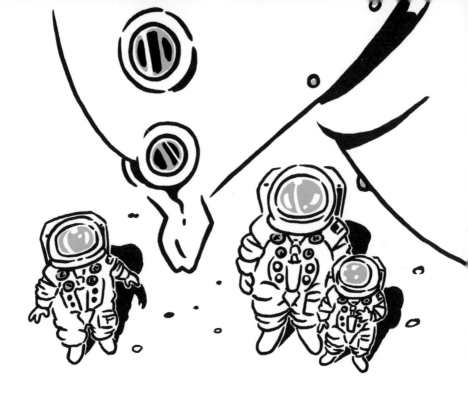

"Moon suits, everyone," said Albert Hopper.

They went outside. The ship's beak was bent.

"We can knock that back in place," said the professor. "We'll be on our way in no time!"

"Can we wait?" asked Tad.

"Why?" asked Polly.

"Look," said Tad. The big, beautiful blue planet called Earth shone in the darkness of space. "I think that one's my favorite," said Tad.

"I agree," said Polly.
"As do I, my niece."
"Thanks," said Earth.

Polly's Notes –

LONG TRIP! 4 billion miles from the sun to DWARF Planet Pluto. (Then a million more miles into the KUIPER BELT.) And back again.

But I LOVE OUR SOLAR SYSTEM!!!

• SUN – Big! It could hold a million Earths! Its gravity keeps our planets orbiting around it, and it gives us warmth and light. My favorite star!

• MERCURY – Smallest planet, closest to the sun. 2-month-long days are SUPER hot. 2-month-long nights are SUPER cold.

• VENUS – 2nd closest to the sun. Surface is hidden beneath clouds . . . that are filled with SULFURIC ACID, which can melt LOTS of things!

• MARS – 4th closest to the sun (Earth is the 3rd closest). Looks like an Earth desert, but with pink skies during the day, and blue sunsets.

• JUPITER – 5th planet from the sun. It is . . . HUGE! Could hold 1,300 Earths! The surface is mostly hydrogen and helium, like our sun.

•<u>SATURN</u> — 6th Planet from the sun. Just so beautiful up close! The shiny rings are mostly orbiting ice. We visited its moon <u>Titan</u>. It's a little like Earth, with rivers and lakes, but don't drink from them! Liquid METHANE! Could still be a nice place for a future ~~clubhouse~~ headquarters.

•<u>URANUS</u> — 7th planet from the sun. BIG (3rd biggest), tilted funny (spins from top to bottom), and cold (THE coldest planet).

• <u>NEPTUNE</u> — Farthest from the sun. Also big (4th biggest) and cold (almost the coldest planet). Kind of like Uranus's slightly smaller twin.

•<u>PLUTO</u> — Former farthest "planet" from the sun, but is now called a dwarf planet. Some are not happy about that.

• <u>Uncle Albert</u> — I sometimes think he has a brain the size of Jupiter.

•<u>Tad</u> — He has his moments.